P9-DZY-139

ULTRABOT'S FIRST PLAYDATE

Josh Schneider

CLARION BOOKS Houghton Mifflin Harcourt Boston New York

TO DANA

Clarion Books
3 Park Avenue
New York, New York 10016

Clarion Books is an imprint of
Houghton Mifflin Harcourt Publishing Company.

hmhco.com

The illustrations in this book were done in watercolor,
pen and ink, and Photoshop.
The text was set in Agenda and Joystick.

Library of Congress Cataloging-in-Publication Data
Names: Schneider, Josh, 1980- author, illustrator.
Title: Ultrabot's first playdate / Josh Schneider.
Description: Boston ; New York : Clarion Books, Houghton Mifflin Harcourt, [2019] | Summary: When Ultrabot has his first playdate, he is worried and shy but he soon learns that he and Becky have a lot in common.
Identifiers: LCCN 2018035186 | ISBN 9781328490131 (hardback)
Subjects: | CYAC: Robots--Fiction. | Play--Fiction. | Friendship--Fiction. | BISAC: JUVENILE FICTION / Robots. | JUVENILE FICTION / Social Issues / Friendship. | JUVENILE FICTION / Humorous Stories. | JUVENILE FICTION / Social Issues / New Experience. | JUVENILE FICTION / Imagination & Play.
Classification: LCC PZ7.S36335 Ult 2019 | DDC [E]--dc23
LC record available at https://lccn.loc.gov/2018035186

Manufactured in China
SCP 10 9 8 7 6 5 4 3 2 1
4500755875

5
5
5

Ultrabot lived with its professor in a little top-secret laboratory on Primrose Lane.

One day, the professor got a phone call.

"Ultrabot," said the professor, hanging up the phone. "Tomorrow is a big day. Do you know why?"

"**NEGATIVE**," said Ultrabot.

"Tomorrow, Becky Tingle from next door is coming over for a playdate. Won't that be fun?"

"**NEGATIVE**," said Ultrabot.

"That's not a very positive attitude," said the professor.

B2
5
PROFESSOR

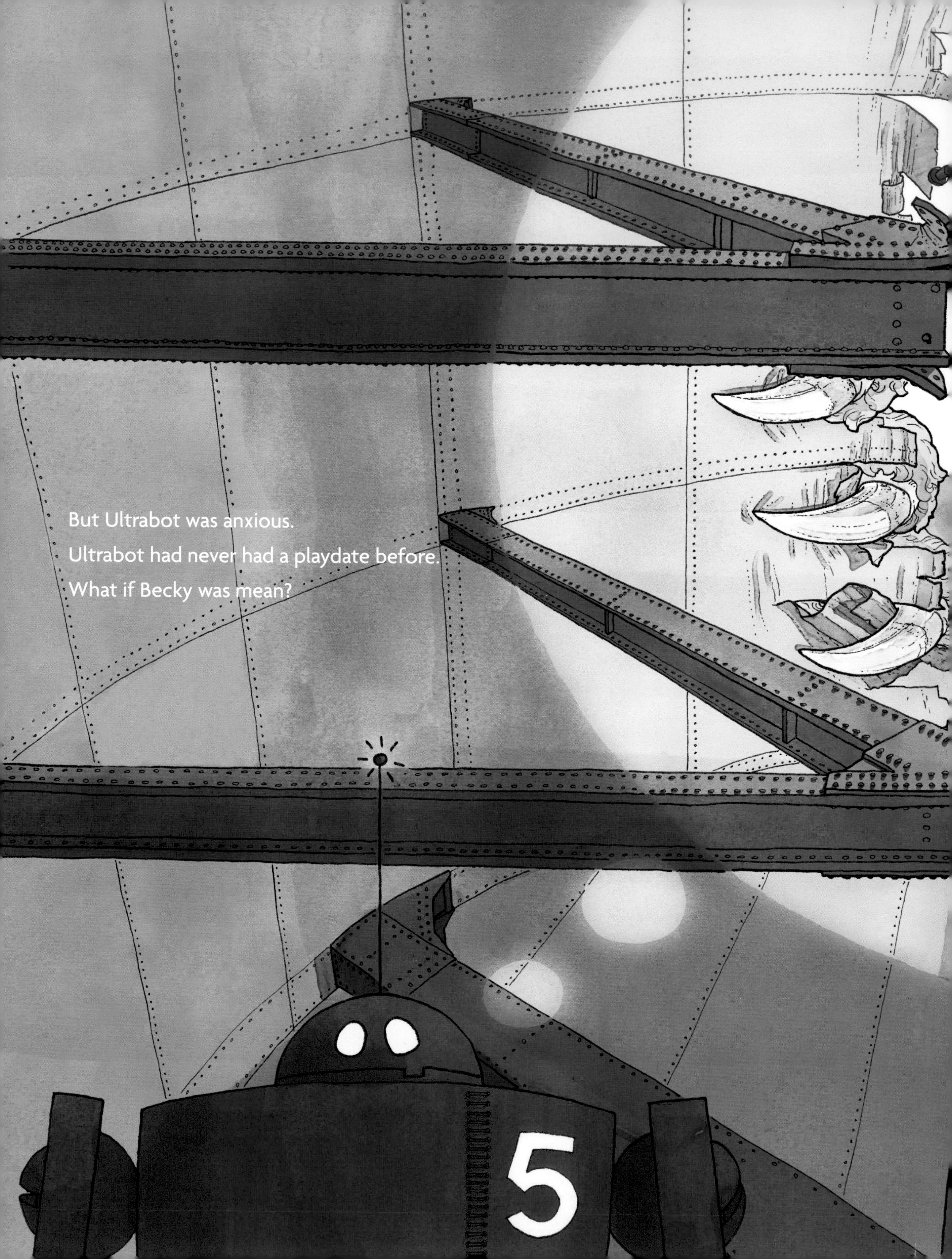

But Ultrabot was anxious.
Ultrabot had never had a playdate before.
What if Becky was mean?

HELLO
MY NAME IS
Becky

What if she broke all of Ultrabot's toys?
Ultrabot would have nothing to play with!

D8
DANA

That night, Ultrabot had trouble sleeping.

5
5

The next day, the doorbell rang.

It was Mrs. Tingle from next door.

And Becky.

"Say hello, Becky," said Mrs. Tingle.

"Hello," said Becky.

"Say hello, Ultrabot," said the professor.

"HELLO," said Ultrabot.

HELLO,
SHALL WE PLAY
A GAME?
Y/N
5
M
Tu
W
Th
F
5

Ultrabot was shy at first.

But Becky had a ball.

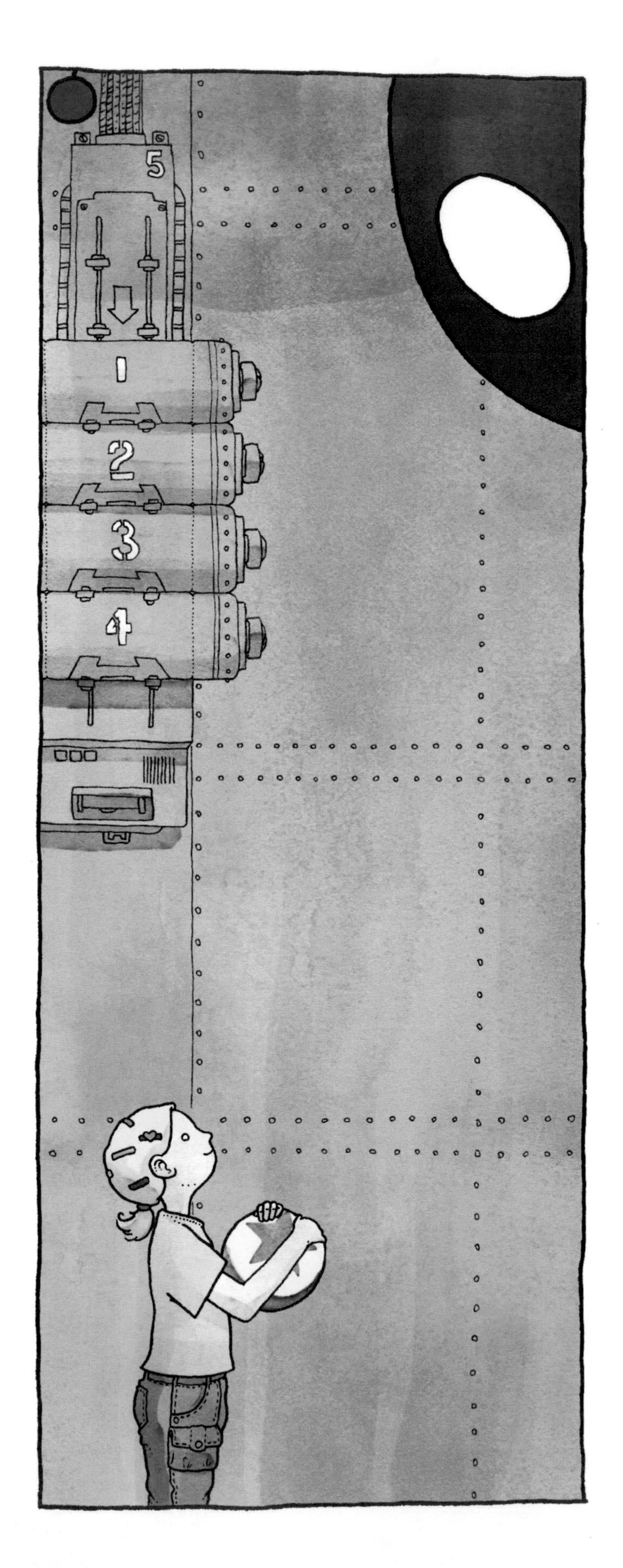

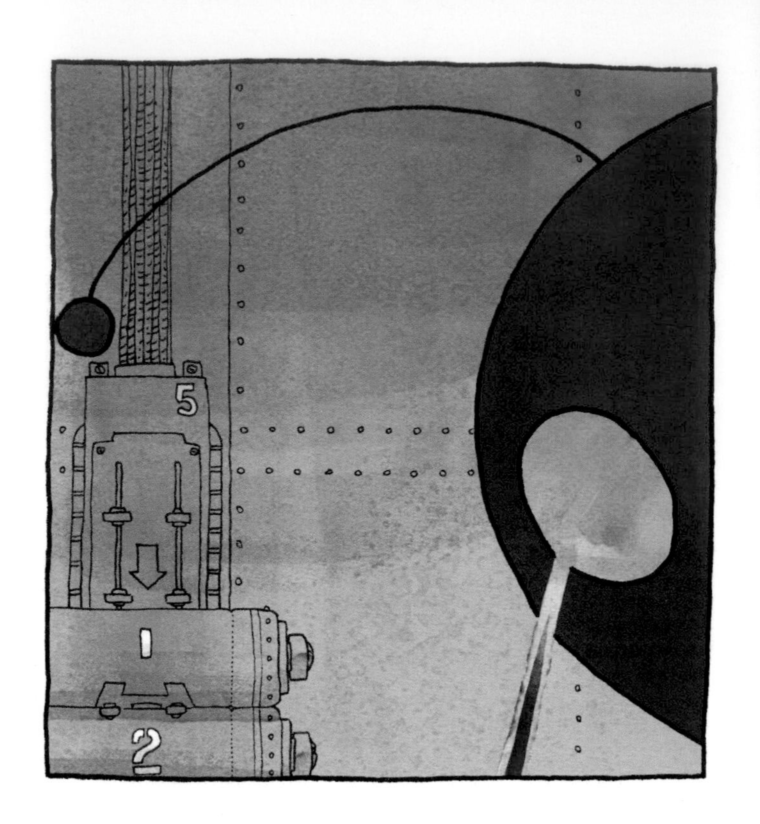

It looked pretty great.

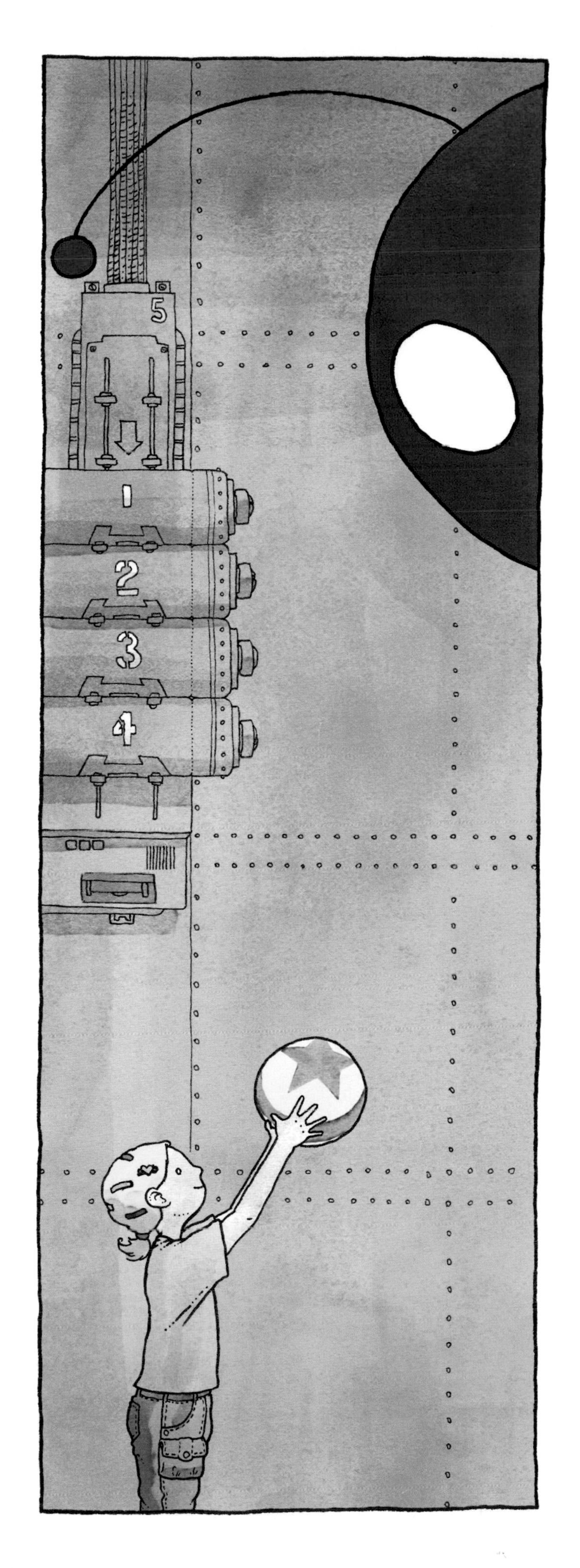

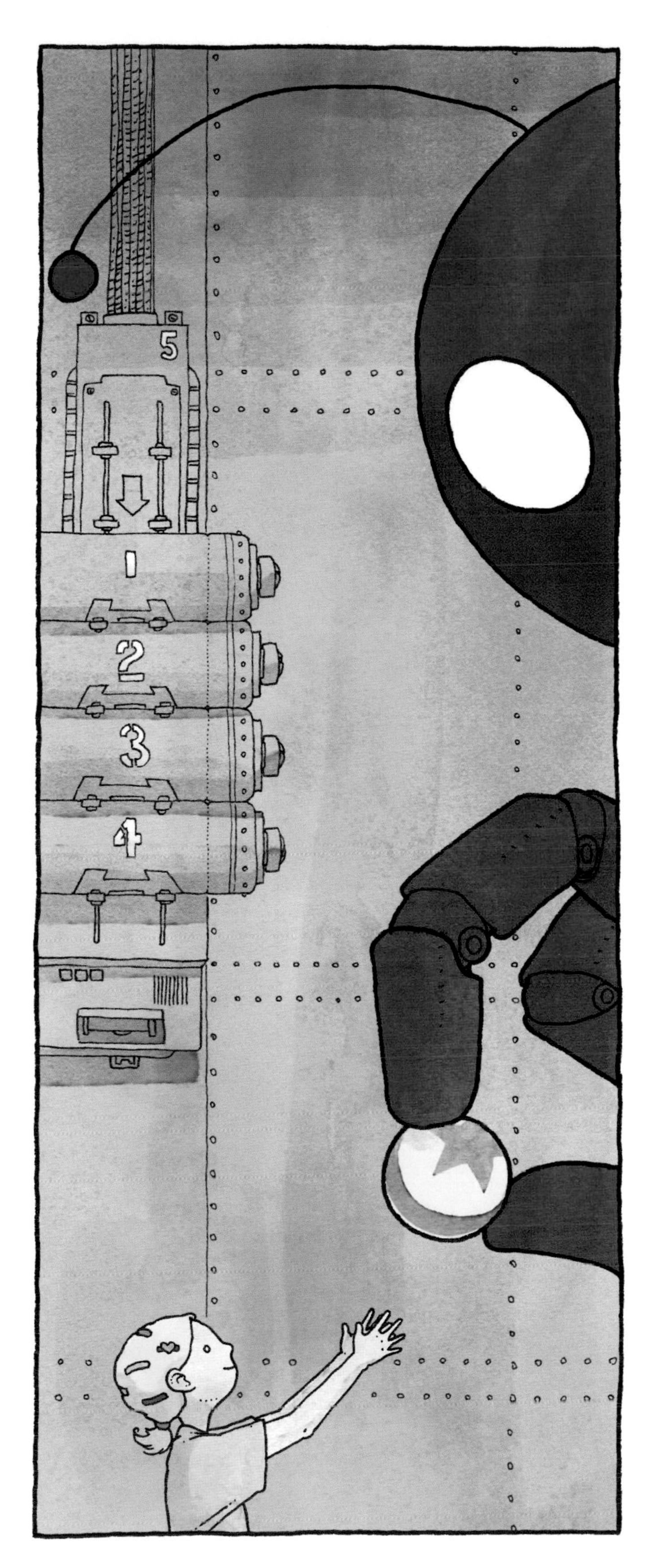

And Becky was willing to share.

They had a contest to see who could bounce
Becky's ball the most times in one try.

1
2
3
4
5
6
7
8
9
10
11
12
13
14
15
16
17
18
19
5

1%
5

Becky showed Ultrabot how to draw a cat.

The professor made sandwiches for lunch.
Ultrabot and Becky both liked their crusts cut off.
They had a lot in common.

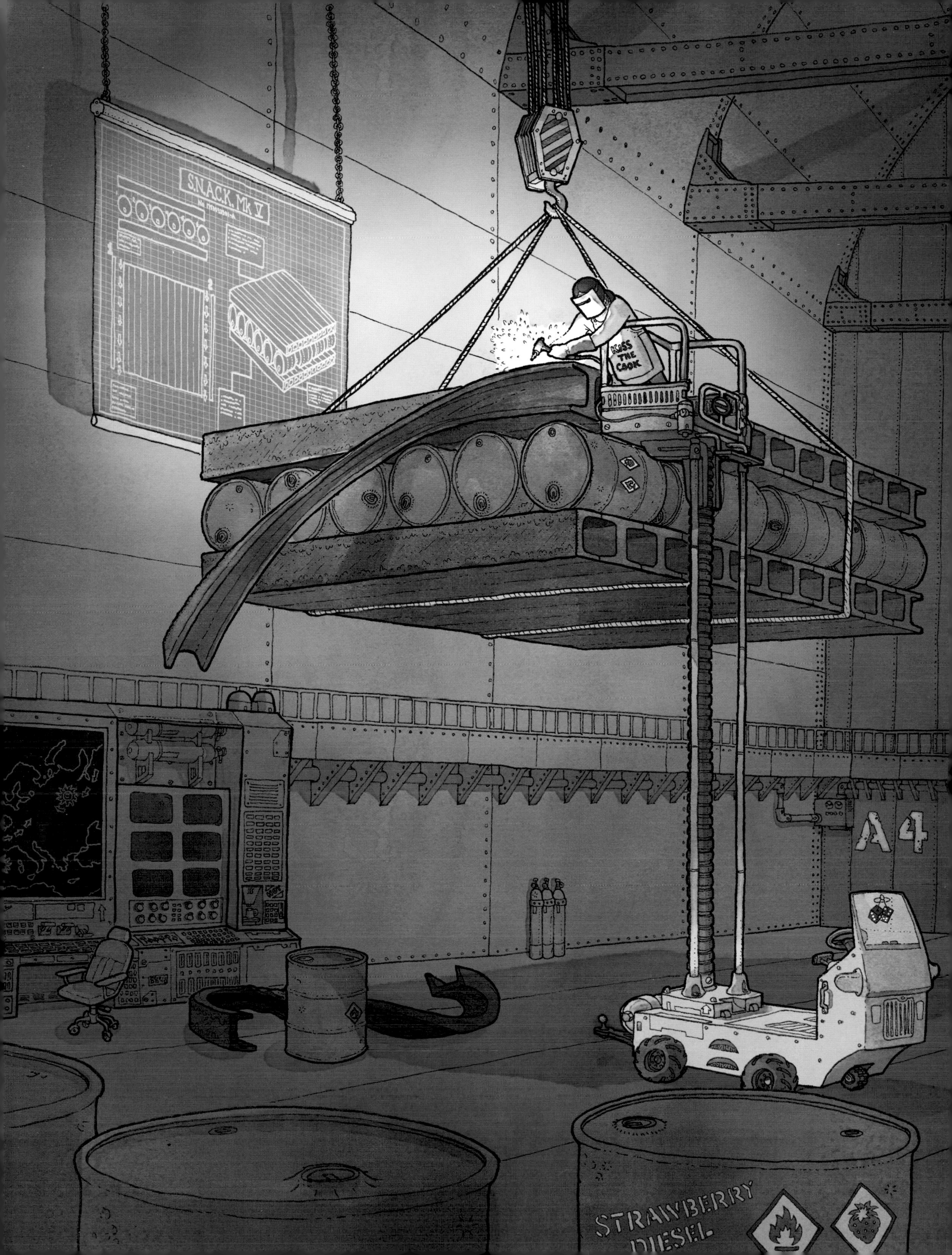
S.N.A.C.K. Mk V
KISS THE COOK
A4
STRAWBERRY DIESEL

Ultrabot decided it was safe to share its toys with Becky, too.

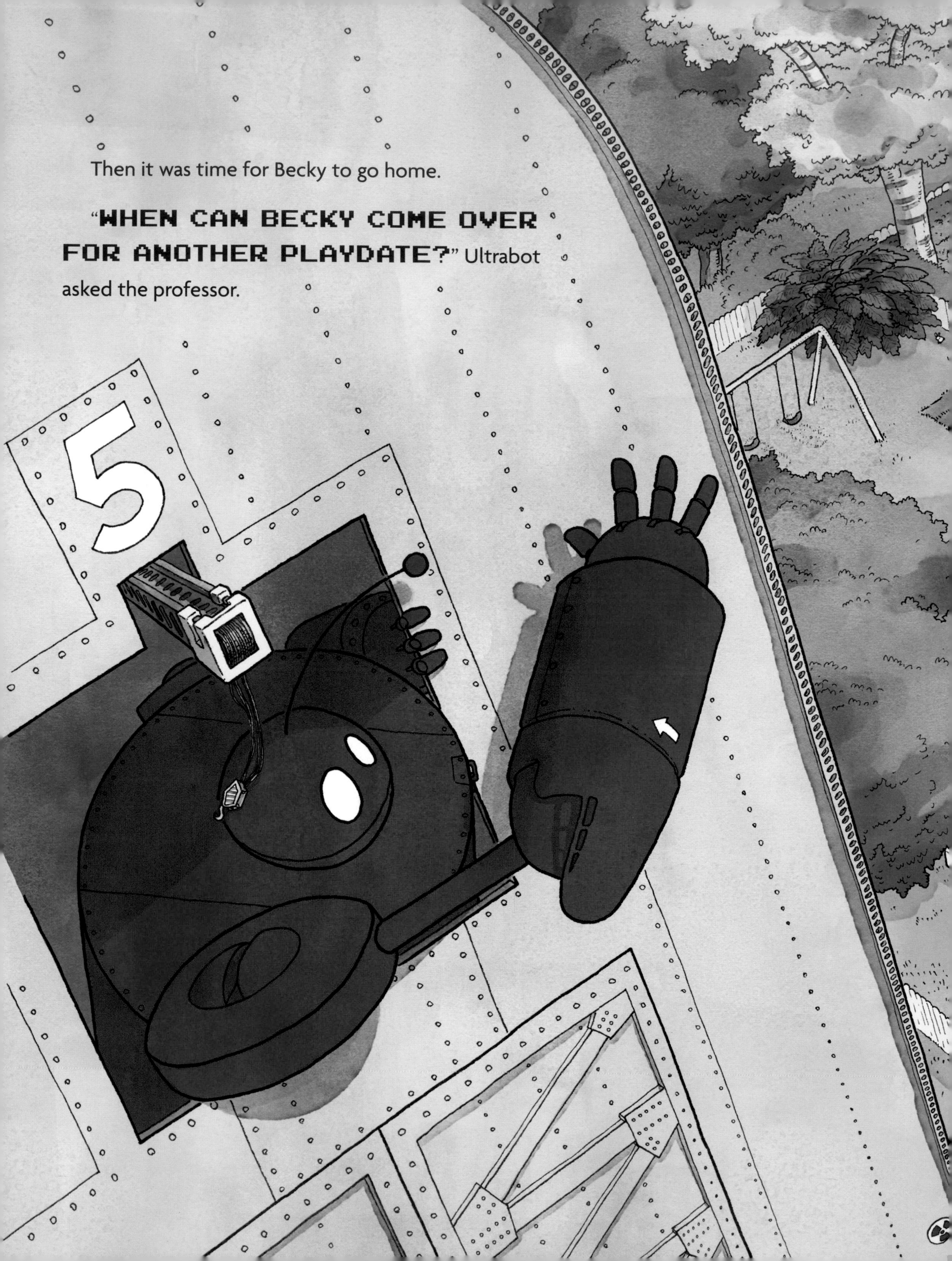

Then it was time for Becky to go home.

"**WHEN CAN BECKY COME OVER FOR ANOTHER PLAYDATE?**" Ultrabot asked the professor.

"Maybe next time you can go to Becky's house," said the professor.

Ultrabot could hardly wait.

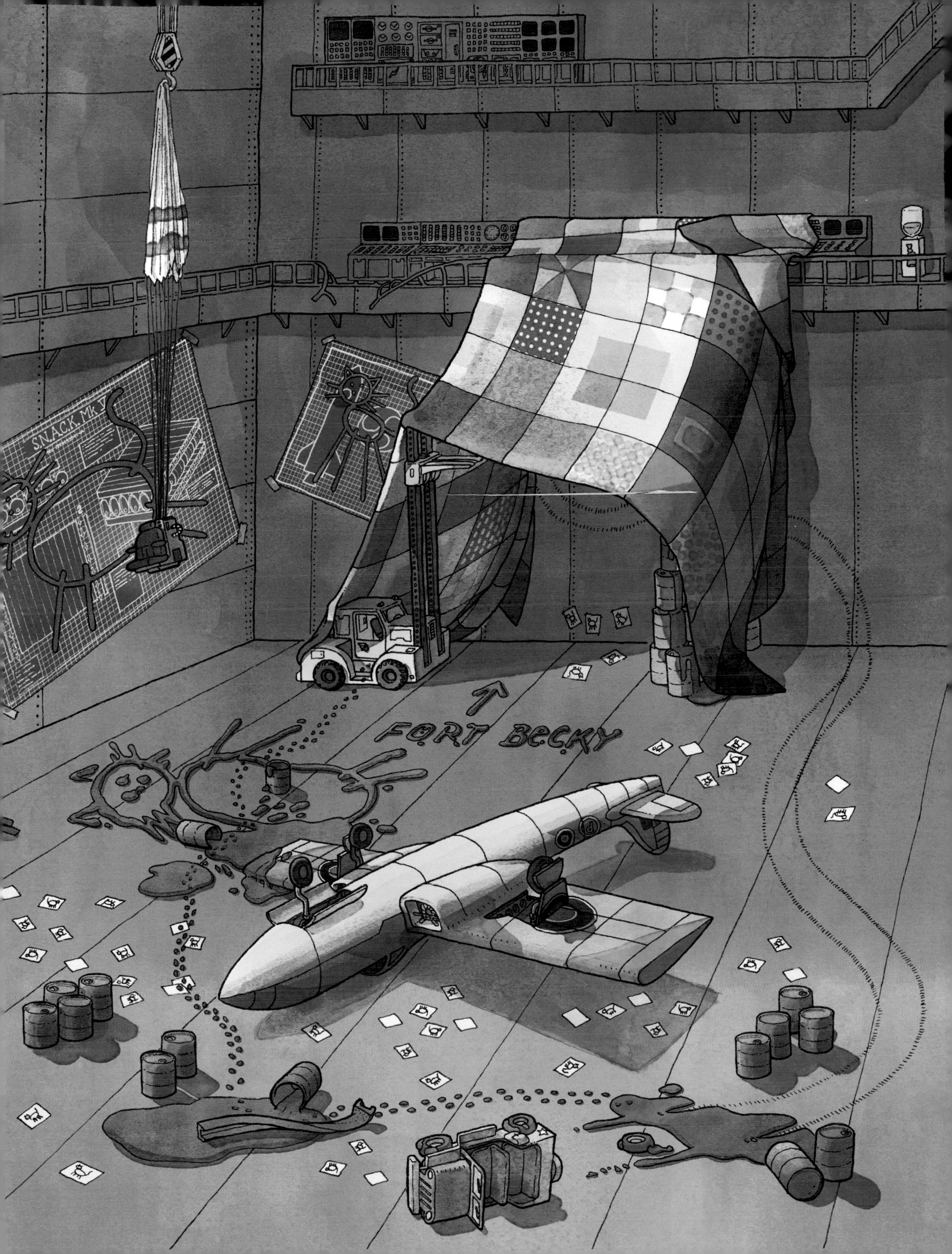
S.N.A.C.K. Mk V
FORT BECKY

BECKY